MW01013659

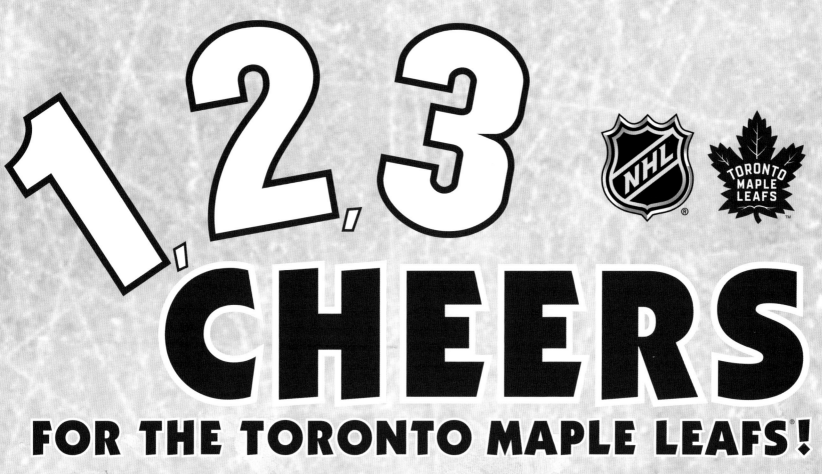

1, 2, 3 CHEERS

FOR THE TORONTO MAPLE LEAFS®!

An Official Toronto Maple Leafs® Book of Numbers

Matt Napier *Illustrated by* Melanie Rose

GO LEAFS GO

Memories made in one hundred years,
with smiling crowds and joyous cheers.
Let's count our way through history,
and where to start's no mystery . . .

1

ONE team stands above the rest:
the Maple Leafs are the league's best.
Jump out of your seat and clap your hands!
No city can beat Toronto's fans.

Toronto's hockey team was founded in 1917 and was originally named the Toronto Arenas. The team got off to a great start by winning the Stanley Cup Championship in their first year in the NHL!

2

The players standing proud and tall,
wearing jerseys beloved by all.
The Maple Leafs crest shines so bright,
with the **TWO** famous colours – blue and white.

The Leafs have changed the style of the maple leaf logo on their jersey several times throughout the years. But one thing has never changed since the Toronto hockey team's first season as the Maple Leafs in 1927 – the iconic blue and white colours.

3

Did you know there have been THREE team names in Toronto history? The Maple Leafs, but before that, the Toronto Arenas and the St. Pats.

In 1919, the Toronto Arenas became the St. Pats, winning the Stanley Cup in 1922. In 1927, Conn Smythe took over management of the team, and it was renamed the Maple Leafs. Smythe said that the badge represented "pride, honour and courage" and served as a reminder of the sacrifices made by Canadian soldiers, who wore the maple leaf on their uniforms, in World War One.

SALMING 1

SITTLER 2

STANLEY 3

SUNDIN 4

4

Salming, Sittler, Stanley, Sundin.
Between them, is there a common theme?
These **FOUR** Leafs are stars, no less,
and their names begin with the letter S!

Borje Salming, Darryl Sittler, Allan Stanley and Mats Sundin are among the best players to ever wear a Leafs jersey. Each of these greats was a perennial all-star during his career and all are members of the Hockey Hall of Fame. Allan Stanley was also a key member of the Maple Leafs teams that won four Stanley Cup Championships in six years during the 1960s.

5

In the rafters, you can spy
retired numbers way up high.
Barilko's **FIVE** shall always slumber.
No other Leaf can wear that number.

Bill Barilko only played five seasons in the NHL, from
1947 to 1951, all with Toronto, but in that time he won
four Stanley Cup Championships. In 1951, he scored
the Stanley Cup–winning goal in overtime against the
Montreal Canadiens and cemented his place as a Toronto
legend. Barilko's number 5 and Ace Bailey's number 6 are
the only two numbers retired by the team.

6

When the young NHL was finding its feet,
watching the games was really a treat.
Just a few other clubs were in the mix;
the Leafs are one of the Original **SIX.**

The NHL was a six-team league for twenty-five years
between 1942 and 1967. That period is the longest stretch
of time that the NHL has featured the exact same group
of teams. The Original Six teams are the Montreal
Canadiens, the Boston Bruins, the Detroit Red Wings,
the Chicago Blackhawks, the New York Rangers and,
of course, the Toronto Maple Leafs.

7

Waking up early to take you to the rink,
Mom and Dad need a coffee to drink.
They take one sip, and it tastes like heaven.
Remember Tim Horton and his number **SEVEN?**

Long before Tim Hortons was an iconic Canadian institution, Toronto fans knew its cofounder as their star defenceman. Horton played on the Maple Leafs for twenty seasons and won four Stanley Cup Championships wearing number 7. He opened the first restaurant (then called Tim Horton Donuts) with his business partner, Ron Joyce, in Hamilton in 1964. Tim Hortons is now an international restaurant with over 3,500 locations in Canada alone!

In '72, Leafs fans were elated,
cheering their hero, while Canada celebrated.
Paul Henderson scored – wasn't that great?
To beat the Soviets in game number **EIGHT.**

The 1972 Summit Series was a competition played between Canada and the Soviet Union. There were eight games – four in Canada and four in the Soviet Union. Going into the last game in Moscow, the teams were tied. Paul Henderson, who played in the NHL for the Maple Leafs, scored with thirty-four seconds left in the third period to win the series for Canada.

9

NINE times the Leafs were able to say their rookie was better than any other to play and won this award to start his career: It's the Calder Trophy for Rookie of the Year.

The Calder Memorial Trophy is awarded every year to the best rookie in the NHL. The award is named after Frank Calder who was the first president of the NHL. The Leafs who have won the Calder Trophy are: Syl Apps (8), Gus Bodnar (5), Kent Douglas (3), Dave Keon (1), Frank Mahovlich (9), Frank McCool (7), Howie Meeker (2), Brit Selby (6) and Gaye Stewart (4).

10

Quick, a quiz! Can you name
the Leaf with **TEN** points in just one game?
Here, come see! Now take a look
at Darryl Sittler in the record book.

On February 7, 1976, Darryl Sittler scored ten
points in a game against the Boston Bruins
(six goals and four assists). To this day, it remains
the record for the number of points scored by a
single player in a single NHL hockey game.

11

Let's try to draw our favorite crest —
it's the leaf that we love the best.
Up and down we trace the lines,
which come to a point **ELEVEN** times.

Before adopting the current maple leaf design with 31 points, the maple leaf had eleven points. The 11-point maple leaf was introduced in the 1967 season and was influenced by the Canadian flag, which had been established a few years earlier and also had a maple leaf with 11 points.

BOWER 1   KELLY 4   BARILKO 5   BAILEY 6   HORTON 7   KENNEDY 9   ARMSTRONG 10   SUNDIN 13   CLARK 17   SALMING 21   SITTLER 27   GILMOUR 93

12

TWELVE different numbers hanging side by side,
filling Toronto fans with lots of pride.
Read the names along with me —
they are the best in Leafs' history.

In the rafters at the Air Canada Centre you can see banners with the names and numbers of the Maple Leafs' honoured members. A total of eighteen legendary Leafs have been honoured this way: Syl Apps (10), George Armstrong (10), Ace Bailey (6), Bill Barilko(5), Johnny Bower (1), Turk Broda (1), King Clancy (7), Wendel Clark (17), Charlie Conacher (9), Hap Day (4), Doug Gilmour (93), Tim Horton (7), Red Kelly (4), Ted Kennedy (9), Frank Mahovlich (27), Borje Salming (21), Darryl Sittler (27), and Mats Sundin (13).

STANLEY CUP CHAMPIONS

1918 1922 1932 1942
1947 1948 1932 1949 1951
1963 1964 1949 1951 1967

TORONTO MAPLE LEAFS

TORONTO MAPLE LEAFS

13

Speaking of records that make us cheer,
here is one that we hold dear:
It's been **THIRTEEN** times we've won the Cup —
a number we hope will go up and up!

Toronto has won thirteen Stanley Cup
Championships – one as the Toronto Arenas,
one as the Toronto St. Patricks and eleven as
the Maple Leafs.

14

In the dressing room, the players prepare,
putting on the equipment they all must wear.
Look really hard, this will be fun.
There are **FOURTEEN** pieces – can you spot each one?

Can you find all fourteen pieces of equipment?
There are two skates, two shin pads, a protective
cup, pants, shoulder pads, two elbow pads, two
gloves, a neck guard, a helmet and a stick – all
adding up to fourteen!

15

In overtime, the score is tied.
The pressure's on; there's nowhere to hide.
FIFTEEN times Sundin saved the day,
scoring a goal and leading the way.

When Mats Sundin retired in 2009, he held the NHL record with fifteen career overtime game-winning goals. Sundin played thirteen years for Toronto, serving as captain for eleven. He is the Toronto Maple Leafs all-time leader in career points (987) and goals (420).

Don't stop now; we've come so far!
You know your numbers – you're a counting star!
Let's turn the page and count some more.
There many more Leafs numbers in store . . .

20

Air Canada Centre is an exciting place.
Across the ice, the visitors face
a group that gives them quite a fright –
TWENTY players wearing blue and white.

NHL teams dress twenty total players – eighteen
skaters and two goalies. When an opposing team
comes into the Air Canada Centre to face off
against Toronto, they are playing against twenty
players proudly wearing Maple Leafs sweaters.

25

At age TWENTY-FIVE, they achieved a great feat:
the Leafs gave Detroit a Stanley Cup defeat.
Down three to zero, fans thought it was done.
The Leafs took the next four, came back and won.

In 1942, the twenty-fifth anniversary of the Toronto franchise, the Maple Leafs won the Stanley Cup in spectacular fashion. After falling behind to Detroit 3–0, the Leafs won the next four games in a row and lifted the Stanley Cup. It remains the only time in Stanley Cup Final history that a team has rallied to win after being down three games to nothing.

30

This duo was a coach's dream.
The two best goalies on your team.
"The China Wall" and **"THIRTY"** stopped the puck —
it's Johnny Bower and Terry Sawchuck.

From 1964 to 1967, the Leafs had the two best goalies in the world splitting time in net. Johnny Bower's nickname was "The China Wall" and he played with the Leafs from 1958 to 1970, winning four Stanley Cup Championships. Terry Sawchuck wore number 30 and played three seasons in Toronto, winning the Stanley Cup in 1967 and sharing the Vezina Trophy with Johnny Bower in 1965.

40

On the radio for **FORTY** years,
his voice sent directly to your ears.
Everyone listened when Foster roared
his famous call: "He shoots, he scores!"

Foster Hewitt was the first commentator for Hockey Night
in Canada on the radio when the CBC program began in
1931. Hewitt was the voice of the Maple Leafs on the radio
until 1971, a remarkable total of forty years! He also spent
some time as the Leafs' TV play-by-play announcer and
called the famous Summit Series in 1972. Foster Hewitt is an
Honoured Member of the Hockey Hall of Fame in the
Builders' Category.

50

Do you know how many Leafs greats
lit the lamp at a really high rate?
FIFTY goals in one year is no easy test,
Rick Vaive is one – can you name the rest?

Rick Vaive was the first player to score fifty goals in one season as a member of the Maple Leafs, a feat he accomplished three times (1981–82, 1982–83 and 1983–84). The other two are Gary Leeman (1989–90) and Dave Andreychuck (1993–94).

60

Before games at the Air Canada Centre, this was the arena that fans would enter to see our players perform great feats: The Gardens at **SIXTY** Carlton Street.

Maple Leaf Gardens was home to the Maple Leafs from 1931 until 1999, a period during which the Leafs won eleven Stanley Cup Championships. The arena also hosted the first official NHL All-Star Game, two of the 1972 Summit Series games and even an Elvis Presley concert among many, many other memorable events! The street on which the Gardens still stands was the inspiration for the name of the Leafs mascot, Carlton the Bear.

70

In the post-season, these two were the best.
They have more points than all the rest.
Gilmour and Sundin really did shine,
scoring a goal or assist at least **SEVENTY** times.

Only two players in Toronto Maple Leafs history have totaled seventy or more total points in the Stanley Cup Playoffs. Mats Sundin had seventy and Doug Gilmour finished his career with seventy-seven playoff points.

80

If we can't get a ticket, but want to be near,
at Maple Leaf Square we'll gather and cheer.
It's the second best place to being inside –
the screen in the square is **EIGHTY** feet wide!

Outside the Air Canada Centre is an area known as Maple Leaf Square. There you can find restaurants and a gigantic TV screen where fans get together to watch the games.

90

The tension is building . . . and then the Leafs score!
The crowd erupts and we let out a ROAR!
It's more than **NINETY** decibels of ear-splitting sound.
We jump out of our seats – high fives all around!

The sound of fans cheering in the Air Canada Centre often goes beyond one hundred decibels – that's about as loud as a jackhammer or a plane taking off!

100

Now at the end, it's been lots of fun.
We counted to a hundred after starting at one.
To the Toronto Maple Leafs, the team we adore:
Happy **ONE HUNDRED** years —
here's to one hundred more!

Dedicated to Richard Cordick, the biggest Leafs fan I know, and his wife, Rae Anne, who endures his obsession. — MN

To my dearest friend C.J.: a good sport in everything, including life.
You were the epitome of kindness, grace, passion and generosity. You are missed. — MR

Library and Archives Canada Cataloguing in Publication is available upon request

Published in Canada by FENN/Tundra, a division of Random House of Canada Limited, a Penguin Random House Company.
Published in the United States by Tundra Books of Northern New York, P.O. Box 1030, Plattsburgh, New York 12901.

Library of Congress Control Number is 2016934896

ISBN: 978-1-77049-801-3
ebook ISBN: 978-1-77049-803-7

Designed by Jennifer Lum

Printed and bound in China

FENN/Tundra Books,
a division of Random House of Canada Limited,
a Penguin Random House Company
www.penguinrandomhouse.ca

1   2   3   4   5   20   19   18   17   16